Cassandra

ANIMAL PSYCHIC

#2

OUT ON A LIMB

Isabelle Bottier
Hélène Canac

Graphic Universe™ • Minneapolis

Thank you, Isabelle, for bringing me on board another beautiful, touching story. It's always a pleasure. And a big, big thank you to my favorite little hedgehog for the illustrations in Jade's apartment! —Hélène

Story by Isabelle Bottier
Illustrations by Hélène Canac
Coloring by Drac

First American edition published in 2020 by Graphic Universe™

Published by arrangement with Steinkis Groupe

Translation by Norwyn MacTire

Graphic Universe™
An imprint of Lerner Publishing Group, Inc.
241 First Avenue North
Minneapolis, MN 55401 USA

For reading levels and more information, look up this title at www.lernerbooks.com.

Main body text set in Andy Std
Typeface provided by Monotype Typography.

Library of Congress Cataloging-in-Publication Data

Names: Bottier, Isabelle, author. | Canac, Hélène, illustrator. | MacTyre, Norwyn, translator.
Title: Out on a limb / Isabelle Bottier ; Hélène Canac ; coloring by Drac ; translation by Norwyn MacTyre.
Other titles: Du rêve à la réalité. English.
Description: First American edition. | Minneapolis : Graphic Universe, [2020] | Series: Cassandra: animal psychic ; book 2 | Summary: Fourteen-year-old Cassandra uses her abilities to seek a new home for a dog whose owner is moving to a retirement home, but matching Garrett with a new owner is challenging.
Identifiers: LCCN 2019013452 (print) | LCCN 2019016768 (ebook) | ISBN 9781541582347 (eb pdf) | ISBN 9781541543980 (lb : alk. paper) | ISBN 9781541586932 (pb : alk. paper)
Subjects: LCSH: Graphic novels. | CYAC: Graphic novels. | Psychic ability—Fiction. | Human-animal communication—Fiction. | Dog adoption—Fiction. | Family life—Fiction.
Classification: LCC PZ7.7.B675 (ebook) | LCC PZ7.7.B675 Out 2020 (print) | DDC 741.5/944—dc23

LC record available at https://lccn.loc.gov/2019013452

Manufactured in the United States of America
1-45429-39684-8/12/2019

WUF!
WUF!
VRRRRRR

HI, TRISTAN!
HEY, CASSANDRA.
WANNA GO TO THE
MOVIES TOMORROW?

HMMMMM . . .

A MOVIE FOR TWO?
SOUNDS GREAT.

SUPER! I'LL MEET YOU OUTSIDE THE THEATER. TWO O'CLOCK TOMORROW.

MISS DOLLY!
LEAVE THAT POOR SQUIRREL ALONE.

DON'T BE SCARED.

WELL, THAT'S SOMETHING. I'VE NEVER SEEN ANYONE WALK UP TO A SQUIRREL WITH SUCH CALMNESS.

WHAT'S YOUR SECRET?

WOOF!
THOSE TWO SEEM TO BE GETTING ALONG!

EVERY TIME! MY GARRETT'S A DOG HEARTTHROB. NO ONE CAN RESIST HIS CHARMS.

IT'S BEEN WEEKS SINCE OUR DOGS FIRST PLAYED TOGETHER. MIGHT BE TIME TO INTRODUCE OURSELVES. MY NAME'S MACHA.
CASSANDRA.

WOOF!

WOOF! WOOF!

WOOF!
WOOF!

AAAAHHH!
WOOF!

MISS DOLLY! STOP IT RIGHT NOW!
I'M SORRY. USUALLY SHE NEVER DOES THAT.

COOL IT!

SHE DIDN'T HURT YOU, RIGHT? YOUR HELMET'S NOT BUSTED?
NO, IT'S OKAY. I JUST GOT A LITTLE SCARED.

WAS IT MY SCOOTER THAT SPOOKED HER?
I DON'T THINK SO. THIS IS THE FIRST TIME I'VE SEEN HER REACT THAT WAY . . .

I WONDER WHAT DREW YOU TO THAT GIRL!

NO, CHARLES . . .
WOOF!

IT'S NO USE—
DON'T TRY TO
STOP ME!
WOOF!

DON'T CRITICIZE MY PERFORMANCE, MISS DOLLY. IT'S NOT EASY TO SAY THESE LINES LIKE I MEAN THEM.

HOW WAS YOUR WALK? DID YOU GRAB THE MAIL?

CLICK

I SEE . . .
HEY, HOW'S TRISTAN?

TRISTAN? I DON'T KNOW. IT'S NOT LIKE WE'RE TALKING TO EACH OTHER ALL THE TIME. I'VE GOT **LOTS** OF STUFF TO DO!

OH, YOU'RE CUTE!
WHAT'S UP? HOW'S LIFE
UNDERGROUND?
ZZZ
?

OH, NO. DON'T TELL ME THERE ARE MOLES IN THE GARDEN!
BLEH! THOSE CRITTERS ARE DISGUSTING.

TOMORROW I'M GETTING SOME REPELLENT! I'LL SEND THAT THING PACKING.
PLEASE, BRUNO, DON'T! THE MOLE LOVES YOUR GARDEN.

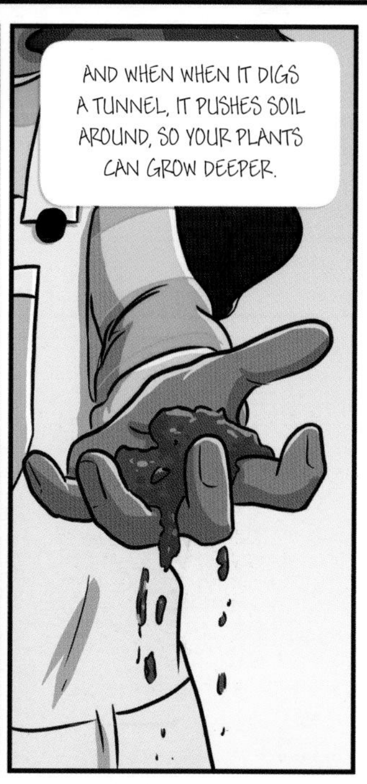
AND WHEN WHEN IT DIGS A TUNNEL, IT PUSHES SOIL AROUND, SO YOUR PLANTS CAN GROW DEEPER.

BLAH, BLAH, BLAH!
PLUS, THE MOLE LOVES EARTHWORMS!

BY EATING **THEM**, IT KEEPS THE WORMS FROM EATING YOUR VEGETABLES.
SURE, BUT IT'S GOING TO FILL MY GARDEN WITH HOLES!

WHAT MAKES IT MORE YOUR GARDEN THAN THE MOLE'S? LEARN TO COEXIST ALREADY!

I . . . NEVER LOOKED AT THINGS LIKE THAT. WHERE DID YOU GET THAT MOUNTAIN OF INFO ON MOLES?

THE MOLE TOLD ME!

I MISS YOU SO MUCH, CASSIE!
HOPEFULLY NEXT VACATION I'LL BE ABLE TO COME AND SEE YOU.

HOW'S SHARING A HOUSE WITH YOUR STEPSISTER?
I DUNNO IF I CAN CALL HER MY STEPSISTER YET. SHE'S JUST BRUNO'S DAUGHTER.

GUESS WHAT?

NO! TRISTAN FINALLY DECIDED TO ASK YOU OUT?

I SEE IT NOW: HE'LL TELL YOU THAT YOU'RE THE MOST BEAUTIFUL CREATURE ON EARTH. HE'LL SMOOCH YOU ON ONE CHEEK, THEN THE OTHER, AND . . . SMACK!

YUCK! STOP!
OH, AND IT'LL HAVE TO RAIN! IN ROMANTIC MOVIES, IT ALWAYS RAINS WHEN THE COUPLE KISSES FOR THE FIRST TIME. IT'S SO DREAMY!

CASSANDRA, YOU'RE SO BEAUTIFUL!

YAAAH!

YOU JUST RUINED MY DREAM!

YOU'RE THE WORST THING THAT'S EVER HAPPENED TO ME!
NOT BAD, BUT I THINK YOU SHOULD PUT A LITTLE MORE ANGER IN IT.
Super Flakes

WHAT ARE YOU DOING?
JULIET'S HELPING ME REHEARSE MY PART IN A SUNSHINE AND CRIMES EPISODE. IT'S THE FIRST TIME I'M GETTING BUMPED OFF IN A ROLE!

YOU'RE GLOWING TODAY. DID YOU DO ANYTHING SPECIAL?
NOPE.

I'M HEADING OUT. SEE YOU TONIGHT!

AFTER YOUR LITTLE SPEECH ON MOLES YESTERDAY, BRUNO ASKED ME SOME QUESTIONS. IT MIGHT BE TIME TO TELL HIM YOUR LITTLE SECRET.
THE PROBLEM ISN'T BRUNO. IT'S JULIET.

SOMETIMES I FEEL LIKE SHE'S JEALOUS OF ME.
SHE'S NOT THAT BAD, YOU KNOW. SHE JUST HAS A LITTLE TROUBLE LOVING **HERSELF**.

SOMEHOW I DON'T THINK TELLING HER I CAN TALK TO ANIMALS WOULD HELP HER WITH THAT.

YOU WOULDN'T HAPPEN TO KNOW SOMEONE WHO'S LOOKING TO ADOPT A DOG, WOULD YOU?
NO ONE COMES TO MIND. WHAT BREED OF DOG? HOW OLD?
IT'S GARRETT!
YOU WANT TO GIVE GARRETT AWAY? BUT . . . WHY?

IN A FEW WEEKS, I'M LEAVING MY APARTMENT TO LIVE IN A RETIREMENT HOME.

I AVOIDED IT FOR A LONG TIME. BUT NOW I HAVE TO ACCEPT THAT I NEED A LITTLE CARE SOMETIMES.

NO RETIREMENT HOMES IN THE AREA ACCEPT DOGS. AND HONESTLY, EVEN IF I HAD THE OPTION, I'M NOT SURE I SHOULD TAKE GARRETT WITH ME. HE'S A DOG WITH LOTS OF ENERGY TO SPEND. HE NEEDS SOMEONE ACTIVE BY HIS SIDE.

SADLY, MY SON HAS A LOT TO TAKE CARE OF ALREADY. TWO GUINEA PIGS AND THREE CATS. HE SUGGESTED I SEND GARRETT TO A SHELTER.

OH NO! ALL THOSE ANIMALS WAITING AROUND FOR SOMEONE WHO WANTS TO TAKE THEM HOME. IT'S SO SAD.
YOU'RE RIGHT, AND I DON'T WANT THAT FOR MY GARRETT.

AFTER ALL THAT GARRETT HAS GIVEN ME, IT'S MY DUTY TO FIND SOMEONE WHO WILL LOVE HIM. BUT I DON'T KNOW HOW.

I'LL HELP YOU FIND A NEW HOME FOR GARRETT.

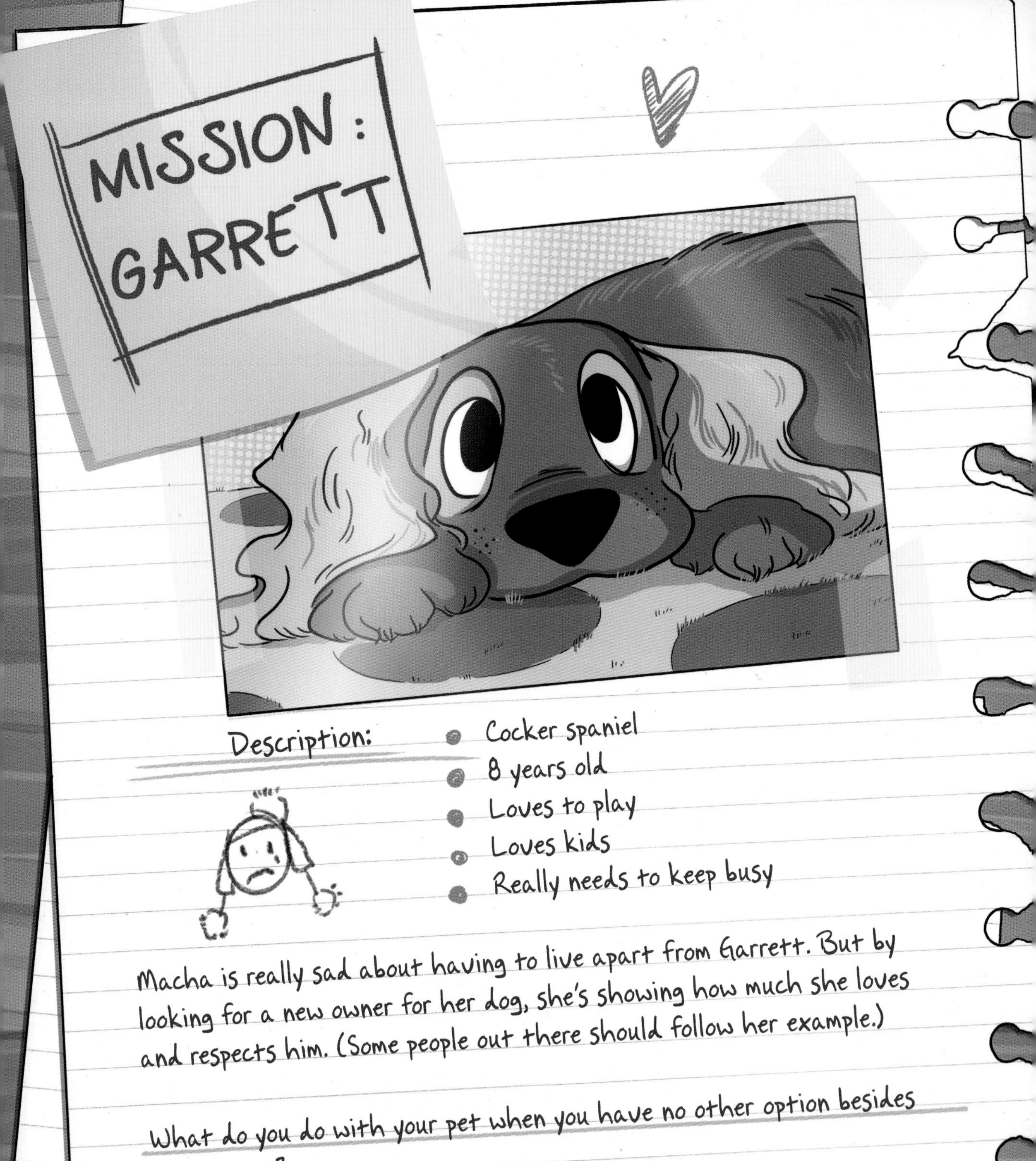

MISSION: GARRETT

Description:

- Cocker spaniel
- 8 years old
- Loves to play
- Loves kids
- Really needs to keep busy

Macha is really sad about having to live apart from Garrett. But by looking for a new owner for her dog, she's showing how much she loves and respects him. (Some people out there should follow her example.)

What do you do with your pet when you have no other option besides giving it up?

You need a good reason to part with your animal—it's not a toy!!!
Feeling abandoned can be an extremely painful experience.

REASONS PEOPLE HAVE TO GIVE UP THEIR ANIMALS:

- The animal has behavior problems
- The person is moving to a retirement home
- A child is born
- The owner passes away
- The owner travels for a long stretch

(Though if you ask me, nobody should be giving up their dog just because they want to go on a big vacation!)

Responsible ways to find your animal a new home:

A SHELTER

At a shelter, your pet will be housed, fed, and cared for as it waits to be adopted. While some animals adapt quickly to these places, others don't do so well.

A RESCUE ORGANIZATION

Pet rescues often put your pet in a foster family until it finds a real family to adopt it. This is ideal for most animals. While waiting to meet a new owner, your pet receives the comfort of a real home.

A POST ONLINE

Some apps and websites offer the opportunity to place pets in new homes. But be sure you practice online safety! With all of these steps, make sure you have the help of a parent or other adults who can make sure you and your pet avoid any unsafe situations.

CINEMA
DONALDSON Plumbers
No mess is too much

THAT MOVIE WAS REALLY GOOD.
YEAH. SUPER!

-CARAMEL
-CHOCOLATE
-PRALINE
-APRICOT
-PEAR
-SAUSAGE
-DOUBLE CHOCOLATE
-PEPPER
-MINT
-PEPPERMINT
-PISTACHIO
-BACON
-CHICKEN
-POTATO
WANT TO GRAB SOME ICE CREAM?

THAT STORY ABOUT MACHA AND GARRETT'S SO INSPIRING. I FEEL LIKE WRITING MY NEXT ARTICLE ON IT. IF YOU WANT, I CAN EVEN PUBLISH AN AD FOR HIM.

SPLASH

ULP! I'M SO CLUMSY.
IT'S NO BIG DEAL.

HEY, IT'S TRISTAN!
BASIL!

WANT TO SIT WITH US?

OKAY, BUT ONLY FOR FIVE MINUTES. I DON'T WANT TO BOTHER YOU.

SO, YOU STILL COLLECTING THOSE ROBO-VAMPIRE ACTION FIGURES?
SHUT UP, THAT'S KIDS' STUFF! WHAT ABOUT YOU? STILL WATCHING NINJA TOONS?

HEH HEH HEH! WE USED TO GET SO CAUGHT UP IN THOSE SHOWS.

I HOPE YOU WEREN'T TOO BORED. BASIL AND I HADN'T SEEN EACH OTHER IN FOREVER.
I GET IT.
FRANKIE'S FISH
WE NEVER FLOUNDER!

HUH! IT'S RAINING.

COME ON, WE'LL KEEP DRY!

CASSANDRA . . . YOU'RE SO . . .

WHOOAA!

UH, NOT A GREAT IDEA TO CUDDLE NEAR A DOOR. THERE ARE LESS DANGEROUS PLACES FOR THAT!

YOU OKAY? DID YOU HURT YOURSELF?
NO!

WHY ARE YOU WALKING SO FAST? WAIT UP!

AAAAAAAAAA...

...TCHOOO!

I'VE GOT TO GO.
THANKS FOR THE DATE.

WUF!
HUSH, DOLLY.
I'M NOT IN THE MOOD.

EVERYTHING ALL RIGHT, MY LITTLE BUG? WHAT ARE YOU UP TO?
I'M MAKING POSTERS. YOU KNOW, TO HELP THE OLD LADY I MET.

I ALSO PUT UP SOME POSTINGS ONLINE.
ALWAYS HELPING OTHERS. I'M SO PROUD OF YOU.

I CAN LEAVE IF YOU WANT TO ANSWER THAT.
VRRRRRR
TRISTAN
NAH, I'M GOOD.

YOU SURE? YOU SEEM A LITTLE MAD. DO YOU . . . WANT TO TALK ABOUT IT?
THERE'S NOT MUCH TO SAY. WE HAD OUR FIRST DATE, AND IT WAS . . . BAD!

OH? DID HE DISRESPECT YOU?

NO!

DID YOU FIND OUT HE'S NOT VERY BRIGHT?

NO!

THAT HE HAS NO SENSE OF HUMOR?

NO!

OH, I KNOW! IT WAS BAD BECAUSE THINGS DIDN'T HAPPEN EXACTLY THE WAY YOU IMAGINED THEM IN YOUR HEAD.

THAT'S NO BIG DEAL!

IT'S TRISTAN. I GOT ALL THE INFO ABOUT GARRETT. THE AD WILL APPEAR TOMORROW . . . AND, UH, SINCE YOU DIDN'T PICK UP, I HOPE EVERYTHING'S GOOD.

COME ON, LET'S PUT UP SOME POSTERS.

AHEM.

WHAT ARE YOU DOING? MOVE THAT BUTT!

THIS ISN'T PLAYTIME. IT'S NOT LIKE I HAVE NOTHING ELSE TO DO!

WOOF!
WOOF!

WOOF!
WHAT'S UP?

SLOW DOWN!
MY POSTERS!

WOOF!
ALL RIGHT, WHAT'S GOING ON WITH YOU? THIS MAKES TWO TIMES YOU'VE ACTED FUNNY WHEN YOU'VE SEEN THIS GIRL.

DOES SHE HAVE A PROBLEM? TELL ME EVERYTHING. TELL ME WHAT YOU FEEL.

THERE'S ONLY JOY AND GOODNESS IN THIS GIRL.

HEY!

SORRY TO BOTHER YOU. WE MET THE OTHER DAY.
OH YEAH. I **DEFINITELY** REMEMBER YOUR PUP.

DO YOU HAPPEN TO KNOW ANYONE WHO'D BE INTERESTED IN A SWEET, GENTLE DOG?
GARRETT'S AN EIGHT-YEAR-OLD COCKER SPANIEL.
I DON'T KNOW . . .

HIS OWNER'S AN OLDER WOMAN WHO'S MOVING INTO A RETIREMENT HOME. SHE'S GOING TO HAVE TO SAY BYE TO HER PUP.
OH, THAT'S SO SAD.

IF YOU CAN SPREAD THE WORD TO YOUR FRIENDS, THAT'D BE NICE. THANKS!

HOLD ON.
I KNOW SOMEONE!

OH? WHO?

ME!

I LOVE YOU, MISS DOLLY!

MY NAME'S JADE. I'M 21.
WILL YOU HAVE ENOUGH FREE TIME TO TAKE CARE OF GARRETT? HE'S A DOG WHO NEEDS TO MOVE A LOT.
I WORK AS A CASHIER AT THE SUPERMARKET. OTHER THAN THAT, I CAN DEVOTE ALL MY TIME TO HIM.
AND I'M PRETTY ATHLETIC. I JOG OR RIDE MY BIKE AT THE PARK A LOT. I CAN DO THINGS LIKE THAT WITH GARRETT.
WHY DO YOU WANT A DOG?
BECAUSE I LOVE DOGS, AND I THINK IT WOULDN'T HURT TO TAKE CARE OF SOMEONE BESIDES MYSELF . . . I GET A LITTLE LONELY SOMETIMES.

I DIDN'T EVEN INTRODUCE MISS DOLLY. SHE'S A VERY GOOD FRIEND OF GARRETT'S.

GRRRR
OOPS, MY BAD! I MEAN GARRETT'S **NUMBER ONE** BEST FRIEND!

I COULD MAKE A LITTLE CORNER JUST FOR HIM. AND THE ADVANTAGE OF A STUDIO APARTMENT IS THAT WE'LL ALWAYS BE IN THE SAME SPOT.

THIS PLACE LOOKS GOOD TO ME . . . I HAVE A FEELING GARRETT WILL BE VERY HAPPY WITH YOU.

YOU ARE SO, SO CUTE. EVEN CUTER THAN I IMAGINED. WHAT DO YOU SAY?

WHAT'S WRONG?
DO YOU WANT TO SIT DOWN?

NO, NO. THANK YOU. IT'S NOTHING.
I'M HAPPY. BUT AT THE SAME TIME, I THINK IT JUST REALLY HIT ME. GARRETT AND I ARE GOING TO BE LIVING APART.

JADE, DO YOU FEEL READY TO GIVE GARRETT THE LOVE HE DESERVES?

I CAN'T WAIT!

YOU SOLVED THAT FAST!
I DIDN'T DO ANYTHING. IT WAS MISS DOLLY. SHE SENSED RIGHT AWAY THAT JADE WAS MADE FOR GARRETT.
IF I HAD KNOWN EARLIER, I WOULDN'T HAVE SPENT SO MUCH TIME MAKING POSTERS. THEY WOUND UP IN THE GUTTER ANYWAY.

AND TRISTAN? YOU STILL HAVEN'T CALLED HIM BACK?
NOPE! I KNOW, IT'S BAD! BUT I DON'T KNOW WHAT TO SAY TO HIM.

IT'S LIKE I FEEL . . . NOT TRICKED, BUT LIKE I BUILT UP A FANTASY OF HIM.
THE DATE WAS THAT BAD?

NO . . . JUST DULL. BUT DEFINITELY NOT ROMANTIC.

THIS BAG HAS ALL GARRETT'S THINGS. HIS BLANKET, HIS TOYS, HIS BOWL.

I'LL LEAVE YOU BE NOW. BE HAPPY, YOU TWO!

WOOF! WOOF!
IT'S HARDER THAN I THOUGHT.

IT'S OKAY.
I'LL TAKE YOU HOME.
TELL ME I MADE THE RIGHT CHOICE.

JADE'S THE PERFECT PERSON FOR GARRETT, I PROMISE. AND I'LL COME TO SEE YOU FROM TIME TO TIME TO GIVE YOU NEWS.
THANK YOU—YOU'RE SO KIND.

IT'S TRISTAN AGAIN. DO YOU NOT REMEMBER ME? DID I DO SOMETHING WRONG?

HAAGADAS

HAVE YOU EVER HAD A BOYFRIEND?
HAAGADAS

TONS!

WELL, ACTUALLY, I ONLY HAD ONE. BUT IT WAS THE REAL DEAL! NOTHING LIKE YOUR SITUATION.

SORRY. I DIDN'T MEAN THAT. IT WAS FIFTH GRADE. HIS NAME WAS JAMES RICHARDS. OUR RELATIONSHIP LASTED THREE MONTHS . . . UNTIL HE DITCHED ME FOR ANOTHER GIRL.

SORRY. DO YOU STILL THINK ABOUT HIM?
YEAH. HE WAS PERFECT!

BUT ISN'T IT SAD TO KEEP DREAMING ABOUT SOMEONE WHO DOESN'T FEEL THE SAME WAY?

LOOK—YOU CAN LOVE SOMEONE ALL YOUR LIFE WITHOUT BEING TOGETHER. AND WHAT DO **YOU** KNOW ABOUT LOVE?

DING DONG
GIVE ME THAT SLIPPER BACK, NOW!

GARRETT RAN AWAY!

HE ESCAPED THROUGH A WINDOW WHILE I WAS IN THE SHOWER!

MAYBE HE'S GOING BACK TO MACHA.
IF THAT'S TRUE, HE'LL FIND A LOCKED DOOR. MACHA MOVED INTO HER RETIREMENT HOME YESTERDAY.

GARRETT'S NOT HERE, AND THERE'S NO WAY HE GOT INTO MACHA'S OLD APARTMENT. EVERYTHING'S CLOSED.

GARRETT!
GARRETT! GARRETT!

IT'S ALL MY FAULT FOR LEAVING THE WINDOW OPEN. I DIDN'T THINK HE'D RUN AWAY.
DON'T WORRY, WE'LL FIND HIM. THE BEST THING TO DO IS SPLIT UP!

GARRETT!

HE'S FOLLOWING MACHA'S FOOTSTEPS!
THERE HE IS!
OH, GARRETT. I WAS SO SCARED OF LOSING YOU. HOW DID YOU KNOW THAT MACHA WAS HERE?
THEY'RE REALLY LINKED TO EACH OTHER.

COME ON, GARRETT. WE'RE GOING!
GRRRR

EASY, GARRETT. JADE ONLY WANTS THE BEST FOR YOU.

MACHA'S BEEN HIS OWNER FOR SO LONG. HE MISSES HER.

DO YOU THINK I'LL BE ABLE TO HELP HIM MOVE ON?
THE GOAL ISN'T TO MAKE HIM FORGET MACHA. IT'S TO GET HIM TO ACCEPT YOU.

HELLO! REMEMBER ME?

I'M SORRY . . .
IF SOMETHING'S WRONG, TELL ME!

GIVE ME SOME TIME . . .
I DON'T HAVE EVERYTHING FIGURED OUT RIGHT NOW.

I'LL CALL YOU BACK. PROMISE.

IF YOU REALLY CARE ABOUT HIM, DON'T LET HIM SLIP AWAY OR YOU'LL REGRET IT!

HERE WE ARE. I FOUND IT!

HERE'S WHERE A CERTAIN JAMES RICHARDS WORKS ON SATURDAY AFTERNOONS.

JULIET IS THE WAY SHE IS, BUT I DON'T WANT HER TO BE SAD.

HAHA! BACK AT YOU, YOU SWEETIE.

WHAT ARE WE DOING HERE?
MARIA ROND
YOU HAVE TO HELP ME FIND A GIFT FOR YOUR DAD'S BIRTHDAY. YOU KNOW HIM THE BEST.

THAT'S TRUE! BUT . . . HIS BIRTHDAY IS IN TWO MONTHS. YOU HAVE TIME!
MARIA ROND
OH, DANG. GOT THE DATE WRONG! WELL, AS LONG AS WE'RE HERE, LET'S TAKE A LOOK AROUND.

COPS VS ROBBERS

JULIET!
JAMES

J-JAMES?

THAT WAS THE FAMOUS JAMES?
YEAH, CAN YOU BELIEVE IT? WE TALKED ABOUT HIM THE OTHER DAY, AND TODAY WE MET HIM!
IT HAS TO BE A SIGN!
AIR RECORDS

AND HE ASKED ME OUT! WE'LL SEE EACH OTHER AGAIN IN TWO DAYS. I WAS RIGHT—WE'RE MADE FOR EACH OTHER!

I'M GOING TO SEE MACHA. YOU WAIT HERE LIKE A BIG GIRL.
ZZZZ
OH! WHAT A SURPRISE!

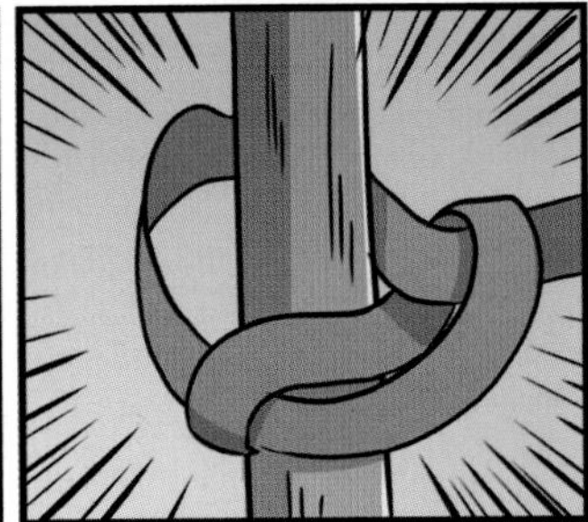

HELP DESK

MY POOR GARRETT. I KNEW IT WOULD BE HARD FOR HIM.

OH, THAT'S A CUTE DOG!

WHAT ARE YOU DOING HERE?

LOOK AT THIS NICE DOGGIE.

SHE'S BEAUTIFUL!
AGNES
REALLY AMAZING!

THAT GENTLEMAN IN THE WHEELCHAIR NEVER TALKS TO ANYONE. BUT TAKE A LOOK AT HOW HE'S ACTING AROUND YOUR DOG. WHAT A GOOD BOY!
AGNÈS
SHE'S A GIRL . . . HER NAME'S MISS DOLLY.

I'M SORRY, BUT OUR RULES ARE STRICT. NO ANIMALS!
TOO BAD. YOU CAN SEE HOW HAPPY THESE PEOPLE ARE TO HAVE A DOG AROUND.
HELP DESK

SO YOUR POLICY SAYS THAT RESIDENTS CAN'T HAVE ANIMALS, BUT CAN THEY HAVE ANIMAL **VISITORS?**
NOT THOSE EITHER.

THERE'S NO WAY TO CHANGE THAT ARRANGEMENT JUST **SLIGHTLY?**
I PROMISE TO TALK TO THE HEAD NURSE AND THE DIRECTOR.

YOU DON'T KNOW HOW LUCKY YOU ARE TO WANT NOTHING ROM LIFE EXCEPT SLEEP AND SNACKS.

SAY, I DON'T SUPPOSE YOU WANT TO TEACH ME TO BE LIKE YOU AND JUST ENJOY THE PRESENT?

TOOT

?

AHAHAH
WAS THAT YOU, DOLLY?

GARRETT ESCAPED AGAIN.
JADE
I DON'T THINK HE WANTS ME . . . AND I CAN'T FORCE HIM TO LOVE ME.

IT'S JUST A MATTER OF TIME. HE HAS TO GET USED TO MISSING MACHA. DOGS ARE REALLY LOYAL.

BE PATIENT AND SHOW HIM YOU UNDERSTAND HIM.
IF HE WANTS TO COME TO THE PARKING LOT FROM TIME TO TIME, LET HIM DO IT.

AND IF HE REFUSES TO LEAVE WHEN WE GET THERE?
THAT'S WHERE PATIENCE COMES IN.

I'M GOING TO GET US SOME SNACKS AND DRINKS.

YOU'RE FINE WITH WATCHING HER WALK AWAY . . . YOU MUST STILL NEED TO WARM UP TO HER, HUH?

DON'T BE AFRAID, GARRETT. MACHA DIDN'T ABANDON YOU. JUST THE OPPOSITE.
MACHA'S LOVE GUIDED YOU TO JADE.
AND HER LOVE WILL ALWAYS BE WITH YOU, THROUGH JADE.
DON'T PUSH JADE AWAY. SHE'S A WONDERFUL PERSON.

SO HOW WAS YOUR DATE WITH JAMES?

HE'S RUDE. AND DUMB.
OH, GREAT. WHERE DID JAMES THE PERFECT GUY GO?

THAT JAMES NEVER EXISTED! I THINK I INVENTED HIM TO FEEL LESS LONELY.

I'M SORRY.
DON'T BE! NOW I'LL BE ABLE TO MOVE ON AND FALL IN LOVE WITH SOMEONE ELSE. FOR REAL.
OH, HI, BETHANY!

JULIET'S HAVING BOY PROBLEMS?
NAH, IT'S NOTHING.

YOU KNOW, BRUNO DIDN'T RIDE INTO MY LIFE LIKE SOME KNIGHT IN SHINING ARMOR. BUT WITH HIM, I'VE NEVER FELT STRONGER OR MORE LOVED.

AND FOR THE RECORD: THE FIRST TIME I MET HIM, HE DIDN'T SEEM LIKE THE MAN OF MY DREAMS.
AND NOW?

IT'S BETTER THAN ANY DREAM.

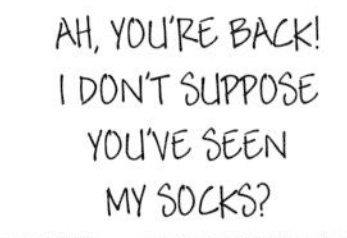
AH, YOU'RE BACK! I DON'T SUPPOSE YOU'VE SEEN MY SOCKS?

I DON'T EVEN WANT TO KNOW WHAT YOU'RE LAUGHING ABOUT.

SOME THINGS CAN'T BE EXPLAINED IN WORDS. YOU HAVE TO LIVE THEM TO UNDERSTAND THEM!

MY NIGHT OUT WITH TRISTAN WASN'T ANYTHING LIKE THE IDEA I HAD OF A FIRST DATE. I THINK THAT SCARED ME.

WELL, BE CAREFUL THAT YOUR IMAGINATION DOESN'T LEAD YOU TO MISS OUT ON SOMEONE SPECIAL.

SOPHIE
TATA
TRISTAN

HEY, TRISTAN. IT'S CASSANDRA.
SCRATCH
SCRATCH

CAN WE SEE EACH OTHER?
WOOF!

THANKS FOR COMING.
ELP DESK

AGNES
WHEN I TOLD OUR DIRECTOR ABOUT THE REACTIONS OUR RESIDENTS HAD TO YOUR DOG, HE WANTED TO SEE IT FOR HIMSELF.

MY GARRETT!

MÉDITATION

THE DOG BRINGS THEM SUCH JOY. IT'S WONDERFUL!

THANK YOU, YOUNG LADY. WITHOUT YOU, WE WOULD HAVE LOST OUT ON SOMETHING IMPORTANT.
HA! YOU CAN THANK MY DISOBEDIENT DOG.

THE WELL-BEING OF OUR RESIDENTS COMES FIRST, SO WE'RE PLANNING TO SET UP A VISITING DOG PROGRAM.

WHAT'S THAT?
SEVERAL DOG OWNERS HAVE AGREED TO COME WITH THEIR PETS A FEW HOURS A WEEK TO SEE OUR RESIDENTS.
150

OH, JADE! IT WOULD BE AMAZING IF YOU COULD DO THAT WITH GARRETT!

THAT WAY, MACHA AND GARRETT COULD KEEP SEEING EACH OTHER.
I'D LOVE TO!

GO AHEAD, GARRETT. GO FIND YOUR NEW PERSON.

CALL HIM.

GARRETT—COME!

THAT'S IT, COME ON, BUDDY . . .

THANK YOU!

IT MUST SEEM KIND OF WEIRD, MEETING HERE.
YEAH, THE PARKING LOT OF A RETIREMENT HOME IS A LITTLE UNEXPECTED.

A FRIEND OF MINE SHOWED ME THIS PLACE. IT'S A SPECIAL SPOT.
LOOK!

OF ANYWHERE IN THE CITY, THIS LOT HAS THE BEST VIEW OF THE SUNSET.
IT'S AWESOME! AND . . . ROMANTIC?

IT'S LIKE YOU.
GLOWING.

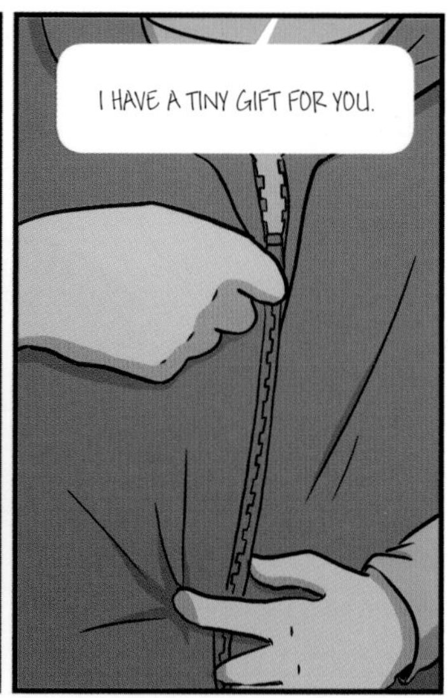
I HAVE A TINY GIFT FOR YOU.

. . . MAYBE I RUINED IT BY PUTTING IT IN MY HOODIE.

A PRESENT!
THANK YOU.

FOR A MOST BEAUTIFUL FLOWER.

YOU'RE SHIVERING! ARE YOU COLD?

NAH. I'M GOOD.

SECRET NOTEBOOK

All about

Miss Dolly

Wait, There's More!

When I was younger and Sophie would come over to hang out, I tended to leave Miss Dolly be. I'd even ignore her as long as my friend was around. My dog didn't like to be stuck in the background, so she was quick to let me know by grumbling about it.

After that, I understood that her reaction was totally my fault. A dog lives by its habits. When something interrupts those habits, the dog can act pretty fussy. So I looked back at how I was acting.

Nowadays, whether it's Sophie or someone else visiting me, I always spend a short moment making some introductions between Missy Dolly and my guest. Depending on the person and what we're planning on doing, I might invite my dog to join us. Warning! Loving your dog, paying attention to her, and wanting her to be happy is normal. But don't make the mistake of thinking of the dog as a baby or another human. You have to have some boundaries too!

The Funny Fears of Miss Dolly
SHE'S A SCAREDY CAT!
She jumps at her own toots!
toot!
ARRRF
VRRRRRRR
She gets scared when she sees the vacuum!
Even stuffed animals can freak her out!

Boo! A Thief!

All dogs like to sneak stuff for themselves, and Miss Dolly is no exception.

But that's because a dog doesn't understand the idea of stealing. If someone wants to drag something in front of Dolly's snout, she'll think there's no reason not to take advantage of it. Unless you explain to her—without a doubt—that she is not allowed.

For things to change, you have to set some rules.

- Don't feed her when you're at the table. If your dog gets used to waiting for food to fall from your dinner plate, she'll end up thinking that everything on the plate's allowed.

- Don't give leftovers directly from your plate to her bowl. Or your dog will think that what you eat is what she eats.

- Don't leave food lying around in places your dog can reach.

- If your dog steals something, don't run after her to get it back. Your dog might think this is a game. And maybe she'll enjoy being chased so much, she'll start it again whenever she can. Wait until she drops the object to get it back.

- Also, make sure your dog has her own things (toys, blankets).

Sleepy Time Anytime

If there's one thing I envy about Miss Dolly, it's her ability to sleep anywhere and in any position!!!

Improvised Birthday Cake

INGREDIENTS

-cooked ground beef
(or wet dog food or tuna . . .)
-dog biscuits

Take a cookie cutter and place it on a plate. Fill the inside with beef, wet dog food, or whatever you're using. Pack it in well. Place the dog biscuits in a bag, and crush them with a rolling pin. Put the crushed biscuits on top of the beef. Now you have a crust! Then remove the cake from the cookie cutter and serve it.

Happy Birthday, Miss Dolly!